TO BECKY
WITH LOVE
FROM
GRAMMA EDIE
XMAS 1990

Raffi Songs to Read™

BABY BELUGA

Illustrated by Ashley Wolff

Crown Publishers, Inc., New York

Published by Crown Publishers, Inc., a Random House company,
225 Park Avenue South, New York, New York 10003
CROWN is a trademark of Crown Publishers, Inc.
RAFFI SONGS TO READ and SONGS TO READ are trademarks of Troubadour Learning, a division of Troubadour Records Ltd.
Manufactured in Italy

Library of Congress Cataloging-in-Publication Data
Raffi. Baby Beluga / Raffi: Ashley Wolff, illustrator. p. cm.–(A Raffi song to read) Summary: Presents the illustrated text to Raffi's song about the little white whale who swims wild and free. 1. Children's songs–Texts. [1. Songs. 2. Whales–Fiction.] I. Wolff, Ashley, ill. II. Title. III. Series: Raffi. Raffi songs to read.
PZ8.3.R124 Bab 1990 89-49367 782.42′0268–dc20 CIP
AC

ISBN 0-517-57839-5 (trade)
0-517-57840-9 (lib. bdg.)

10 9 8 7 6 5 4 3 2 1

First Edition

Baby beluga in the deep blue sea,

Swim so wild and you swim so free.

Heaven above and the sea below,
And a little white whale on the go.

Baby beluga, baby beluga,
Is the water warm? Is your mama home,
With you so happy?

Way down yonder where the dolphins play,

Where you dive and splash all day,
Waves roll in and the waves roll out.

See the water squirtin' out of your spout.

Baby beluga, oh, baby beluga,
Sing your little song, sing for all your friends.

We like to hear you.

When it’s dark, you’re home and fed.

Curl up snug in your water bed.

Moon is shining and the stars are out.
Good night, little whale, good night.

Baby beluga, oh, baby beluga,
With tomorrow's sun, another day's begun.
You'll soon be waking.

Baby beluga in the deep blue sea,
Swim so wild and you swim so free.

Heaven above and the sea below,
And a little white whale on the go.
You're just a little white whale on the go.

Baby Beluga

Words and music by Raffi and Debi Pike

D
A7
Ba - by be - lu - ga in the deep blue sea, Swim so wild and you swim so free.
D
Fine
Heav - en a - bove and the sea be - low, And a little white whale on the go.
G
D
Ba - by be - lu - ga, ba - by be - lu - ga,
E
A7
D.C. al Fine
Is the wa - ter warm? Is your ma - ma home, With you so hap - py?

2 Way down yonder where the dolphins play,
Where you dive and splash all day,
Waves roll in and the waves roll out.
See the water squirtin' out of your spout.

Baby beluga, oh, baby beluga,
Sing your little song, sing for all your friends.
We like to hear you.

3 When it's dark, you're home and fed.
Curl up snug in your water bed.
Moon is shining and the stars are out.
Good night, little whale, good night.

Baby beluga, oh, baby beluga,
With tomorrow's sun, another day's begun.
You'll soon be waking.

4 Baby beluga in the deep blue sea,
Swim so wild and you swim so free.
Heaven above and the sea below,
And a little white whale on the go.
You're just a little white whale on the go.